By Andrew Gutelle
Illustrated by Joy Friedman

A GOLDEN BOOK • NEW YORK
Western Publishing Company, Inc., Racine, Wisconsin 53404

 Library of Congress Catalog Card Number: 90-86023 ISBN: 0-307-00214-4
MCMXCII

Alex loved baseball. Every day after school, he grabbed his mitt and hurried to the park to play catch with his best friend, Danny.

One afternoon Alex and Danny were surprised to see the park filled with kids playing ball. They were wearing matching baseball shirts and caps. The kids were older than Alex and Danny, and there were adults, too.

Alex and Danny watched as the players tossed a large white softball around the field.

The boys approached a man holding a clipboard. They asked him what team they were watching.

"This is a league softball team," the man explained. "The season is just starting. The kids are beginning practice."

"I wish I were old enough to play," said Alex.

The man pulled two forms from his clipboard. He handed them to Alex and Danny. "Our town has a softball league for kids your age, too," the man said. "Give this application to your parents. There are tryouts next week."

One week later Alex and Danny went back to the park to try out for a softball team. They were very excited. They held their applications in one hand and their baseball gloves in the other. In the center of the field stood the man they had spoken to the week before. A woman holding a bat and a ball was standing next to him.

"My name is Sam Brown," the man began, "and this is Wendy Young. We're in charge of today's tryouts." Coach Brown explained that everyone trying out would get a chance to bat, field, throw, and run.

"And everybody who comes today will be on a team," Coach Young added. "The tryouts just help us make sure that each team has a good mix of players."

The tryouts began. Danny's turn came first. Danny fielded every ball thrown to him and even got a couple of hits while batting.

When Alex got his chance to try out, he ran onto the field. The coach tossed him several ground balls. Alex dropped the first one, but he scooped up the others and threw the ball back pretty well each time.

"You have a strong arm," said Coach Young. "I bet you'd make a good outfielder."

Then Alex took his turn at bat. The first few times he swung and missed. On his last swing he hit a ground ball that dribbled in front of home plate. Alex was disappointed.

"The teams will practice for two weeks before the season starts," Coach Brown told Alex. "Don't worry, you'll have time to work on your hitting."

About a week later, while Alex was doing his homework one afternoon, the telephone rang. "I'm Jim Stevens," said a voice on the other end. "I'm one of the softball league coaches, and you're on my team—we call ourselves the Sluggers. Our first practice is next Tuesday after supper. All the players must get a checkup before they can play. Please see your doctor before then. I look forward to seeing you out on the field."

Alex could hardly wait until the next week.

When Tuesday finally arrived, Alex gobbled down his dinner and raced to the park. The field was filled with groups of kids. Alex found Coach Stevens near second base. He was wearing a purple shirt and hat.

As each team member arrived the coach handed him or her a uniform.

Although his friend Danny was on another team, Alex did recognize a few players on his team.

For the next two weeks the Sluggers practiced twice a week after supper. Each time the players tried different positions. Coach Stevens was good at hitting balls to the fielders. Then everyone took turns at bat. The coach was always the pitcher.

After the final practice, the coach talked to his team. "Next week is our first game. I know you want to win, but I want to be sure everyone has fun," he explained. "Remember, no matter what happens, we root for each other. Whether we win or lose, we do it as a team."

On the day of the first game, Alex wore his team shirt to school. He met Danny in the lunch room so they could talk about the game. The two friends would be playing against each other on the field.

Alex's family ate an early dinner that night so they could see him play. Alex's mom and dad sat with the other grown-ups behind the team's bench.

Before the players took the field, Coach Stevens talked to the team. "Our game is seven innings long," he reminded his players. "You will all play the field for at least six outs. And you will all get a turn at bat. Now good luck!"

Alex began the game sitting on the bench. He was disappointed that he wasn't in the starting lineup. Then he remembered what the coach had said at the last practice about team spirit. Alex began to cheer for his teammates.

The Sluggers led by three runs after four innings. As the fifth inning started, Coach Stevens tapped Alex on the shoulder. "Go play right field," he told him.

Alex felt butterflies in his stomach as he trotted onto the field. He saw his parents clapping, and Danny waved from the opposing bench.

The first batter struck out. But the next batter smacked the ball. It bounced past the second baseman—right toward Alex. Alex grabbed the ball and threw it to the second baseman. The runner didn't get past first base. It was a great feeling for Alex. After that, there were no more butterflies in his stomach.

In the sixth inning Alex batted first. He put on a plastic batting helmet and grabbed an aluminum bat. After a few practice swings, he stepped up to the plate.

Alex swung wildly at the first pitch and missed. He swung at the next pitch and missed again. Then he stepped out of the batter's box and took a deep breath.

"Come on, Alex!" his teammates shouted. "You can do it!"

Alex stepped up to the plate again. He let two pitches go by. On the next pitch, he stepped forward and swung.

There was a loud "PING!" as the metal bat struck the ball. Alex began to run for first base. The ball was sailing over the pitcher's head. Danny was playing center field for the other team, and it was Danny who reached up and caught the ball.

Alex was out, but he had hit the ball hard. He joined his teammates back on the bench.

"Great try, Alex," said his friend Judy.

"Thanks," said Alex. His mother waved to him, and his father gave him the thumbs-up signal.

For the last inning, Alex played right field again. The other team didn't score. When the inning was over, the Sluggers had won their first game.

After the game, the two teams shook hands.

"That was a great hit!" said Danny when he and Alex shook hands.

"Yeah, but your catch was even better," said Alex.

The boys laughed and patted each other on the back. Then they walked home together, tossing a ball back and forth.